# For George Williams

First U.S. edition 2009

Library of Congress Cataloging-in-Publication Data
Dunbar, Polly.
Good night, Tiptoe / Polly Dunbar.
— 1st U.S. ed.
p. cm.
Summary: Tilly is putting all of her animal friends to bed
but Tiptoe the rabbit is definitely not sleepy.
ISBN 978-0-7636-4328-7
[1. Bedtime — Fiction.   2. Animals — Fiction.]  I. Title.
PZ7.D89445Goo 2009
[E] — dc22    2009000897


2 4 6 8 10 9 7 5 3 1

Printed in China

This book was typeset in Gill Sans MT Schoolbook.
The illustrations were done in mixed media.

Candlewick Press
99 Dover Street
Somerville, Massachusetts 02144

visit us at www.candlewick.com

Tilly and
her friends
all live
together in
a little yellow
house. . . .

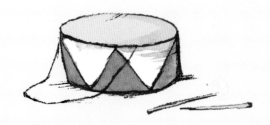

# Good Night,
# Tiptoe

Polly Dunbar

CANDLEWICK PRESS

Hector yawned.

Tilly yawned.

Everybody

**yawned!** Everybody except Tiptoe.

"It's time
for bed,"
said Hector,
snuggling in.

Tilly gave Tiptoe a kiss good night.
## "I'm not sleepy,"
he said.

Tilly helped put curlers in Pru's tail.

"Look who's not in bed," said Pru.

"I'm still not sleepy," said Tiptoe. "I don't want to go to bed."

"You can stay up while I brush
Doodle's teeth," said Tilly.
"Then it's back to bed."

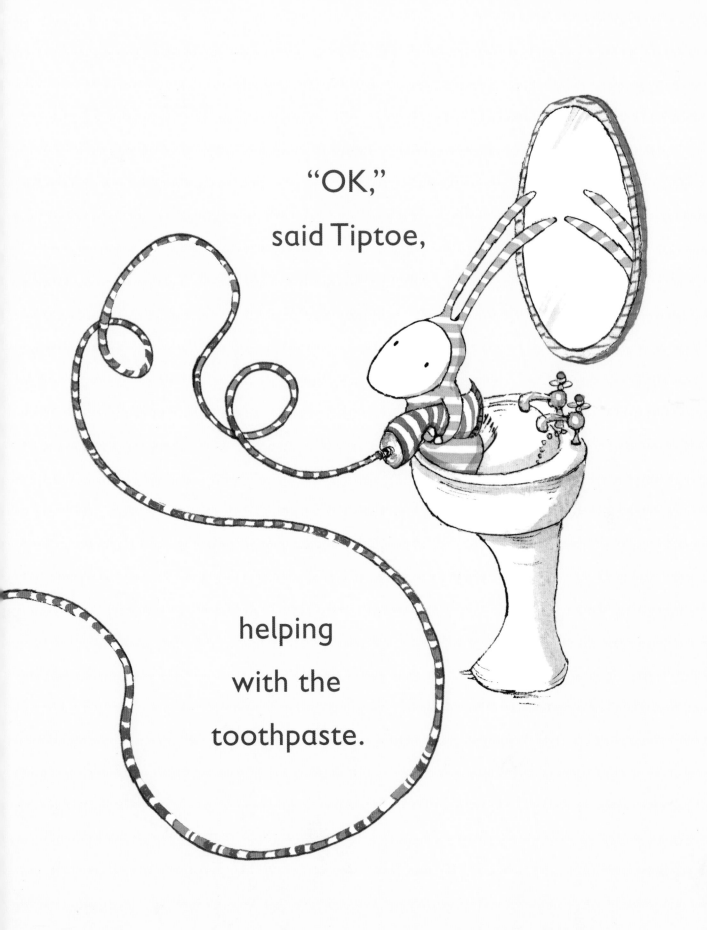

"OK,"
said Tiptoe,

helping
with the
toothpaste.

"Now it **really** is
time for bed," said Tilly.

She sang a lovely lullaby.

T<small>RA</small> L<small>A</small> L<small>A</small> L<small>A</small>

Tiptoe joined in on his drum.

When Tilly
had settled Tiptoe
down again,
she helped Tumpty
with his bath.

"I want a story!"
said Tiptoe.

So Tilly read
a bedtime
story.

Everybody felt very, very sleepy.

Even Tiptoe closed his eyes.

"Sssssshhhh!" whispered Tilly.

"I feel sleepy now,"
said Tilly.
"It must be my bedtime too."
She brushed her teeth
all by herself.

Tilly got into bed
all by herself.
"Who's going to tuck me in?"
she said.
"Who's going to kiss
me good night?"

"I am!"

said

Tiptoe.

Good night!